Woke Babies

The MAGIC Balloon

written by
Carl Anka

illustrated by
Amanda Quartey

This book belongs to

I celebrated World Book Day® 2025 with this gift from my local bookseller and DK.

DK Penguin Random House

Published by Dorling Kindersley Ltd
in association with Woke Babies Ltd.

First published in Great Britain in 2025 by
Dorling Kindersley Limited
20 Vauxhall Bridge Road, London, SW1V 2SA
The authorised representative in the EEA is

Dorling Kindersley Verlag GmbH. Arnulfstr. 124,
80636 Munich, Germany

WORLD BOOK DAY®

World Book Day's mission is to offer every child and
young person the opportunity to read and love books
by giving you the chance to have a book of your own.

To find out more, and for fun activities including video stories,
audiobooks and book recommendations, visit worldbookday.com

World Book Day® is a charity sponsored by National Book Tokens.

World Book Day® and the associated logo are the
registered trademarks of World Book Day® Limited.

Registered charity number 1079257 (England and Wales).
Registered company number 03783095 (UK).

It was a sunny day.
Rosa was in her back garden, playing
football with her best friend, Reuben,
and little brother, Toby.

It was their favourite game
to play together.

THWACK!

'Get ready for the **goal of the year**!' called Reuben.

'Not if I can help it!' said Toby as he put on his goalkeeping gloves.

Reuben kicked the football as hard as he could.

WHOOSH!

Did you see that ball FLY?!

Toby **leapt** into the air.

Rosa gasped as the ball soared past the goal and over the tall fence behind it.

"Yeah, it flew OVER the fence!" said Rosa.

Reuben frowned. "How are we going to get it back?"

Rosa's eyes lit up. "Look! There's a gap in the fence – follow me!"

She led Reuben and Toby to a broken fence panel and they crawled through.

The ball had landed on what looked like a huge blanket. It was made up of all the colours of the rainbow – purple and yellow and green and red and blue.

All of a sudden, the colours began to shimmer and **GLOW** . . .

. . . and the blanket grew **BIGGER** and **ROUNDER**, swelling like a massive bubble.

The football rolled off the top, into Reuben's hands

As the balloon floated upwards, it revealed a big basket beneath it. Inside were three chairs, each with a letter on it: **R**, **T** and **R**.

"That's not a blanket!" said Rosa. "It's a hot-air balloon!"

Reuben, Toby and Rosa climbed into the basket, full of excitement.

As soon as they sat down . . .

A purple flame appeared under the balloon.

The hot-air balloon went up . . . up . . . UP into the air!

The three children stared in wonder at everything they could see.
"Look – it's the **FUNFAIR**!" said Toby.

"There's a **FERRIS WHEEL**!" said Reuben.

"Everything is so tiny from up here!" said Rosa.

The hot-air balloon kept floating onwards and upwards, taking them past their town and . . .

Wow! Is that **THE SEA**?

There are dolphins!

And a seal!

Are we going to **space**? That would be so cool!

Soon, they were high in the sky. **REALLY** high.

Toby yawned. "I want to go home!"

Rosa agreed.
"Come on, Reuben," she said.
"Don't you want to go home too?"

Reuben sighed. "All right . . .
but let's do this again tomorrow!"

As if it was listening, the flame changed
from purple to silver.

I'm really tired.

The hot-air balloon went down . . .
    down . . .
        down . . .
            and landed
                with a gentle bump.

When the children got back
to the garden, Rosa and
Toby's mum came out with
snacks. It was as if they
hadn't been away at all!

The next day, Toby went back through the gap, but . . .
the hot-air balloon was **GONE**.

One bright morning, Reuben, Rosa and Toby were playing
football . . . and the ball flew over the fence once more.

"I'll get it!" said Toby.

He crawled through the gap . . .
and Rosa and Reuben heard him shout:

**"WHOA!
THE BALLOON
IS BACK!"**

Other adventures with . . .

 **DK** and **WOKE BABIES**

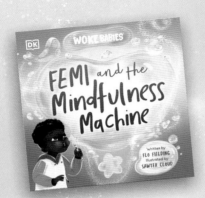

FEMI and the Mindfulness Machine

Written by
FLO FIELDING
Illustrated by
SAWYER CLOUD

WOKE BABIES
The Pond in the Park

Where frogs and friendships grow

Written by
Flo Fielding
Illustrated by
Nathalia Rivera

WOKE BABIES   Smart Senses
BIG NOISE
LITTLE NOISE

WOKE BABIES   Smart Senses
SEEING BIG
SEEING SMALL